S.H. & H. Chapman

Catalogue of the collection of coins of the United States

Ancient creek coins and war medals

S.H. & H. Chapman

Catalogue of the collection of coins of the United States
Ancient creek coins and war medals

ISBN/EAN: 9783742839756

Manufactured in Europe, USA, Canada, Australia, Japa

Cover: Foto ©Andreas Hilbeck / pixelio.de

Manufactured and distributed by brebook publishing software
(www.brebook.com)

S.H. & H. Chapman

Catalogue of the collection of coins of the United States

COLLECTION

OF

COINS AND MEDALS

OF

THOMAS S. COLLIER, Esq.

October 19, 20, 1886.

CATALOGUE

OF THE COLLECTION OF

COINS OF THE UNITED STATES.

AND A FEW

Ancient Greek Coins, and Various Medals

OF

Thomas S. Collier, Esq.,

OF NEW LONDON, CONN.

ALSO A COLLECTION OF

WAR MEDALS.

CATALOGUED BY

S. H. & H. CHAPMAN,

2009 ARCH STREET,

AND TO BE SOLD AT AUCTION BY

STAN. V. HENKELS & CO.

1117 CHESTNUT STREET,

PHILADELPHIA.

TUESDAY AND WEDNESDAY, OCTOBER 19 AND 20, 1886.

COMMENCING AT 2:30 P. M. EACH DAY.

SCALE.

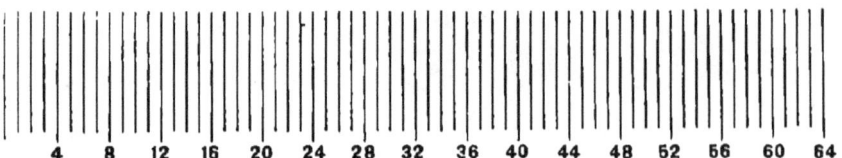

4   8   12   16   20   24   28   32   36   40   44   48   52   56   60   64

CATALOGUE.

--- --

FOREIGN COPPER COINS.

1 Africa. Sierra Leone Co. Prowling lion. Penny, 1791. Bronze proof.
2 Africa. Same device. Cent, 1791. Dull bronze proof.
3 Antwerp. N in wreath. 5, 10 centimes struck by Gen. Carnot while besieged by the Allies, 1814. Fine. 2 pcs.
4 Antwerp. Exposition, 1885. Beautiful token. Bright red.
5 Argentine Rep. Sun. 1, 4 centavos, 1854. Fine. 2 pcs.
6 Australian penny tokens. 2 v.g., balance proofs. Diff. 8 pcs.
7 Australian ½ penny tokens. Uncirculated. Diff. 4 pcs.
8 Bactria. Attributed. 1 Parthian. Fair. 5 pcs.
9 Barbadoes. Negro head. R. Pine-apple. Penny, 1788. Good.
10 Barbadoes. Negro head. R. Neptune. Penny, 1792. V. fine.
11 Bermuda. Geo. III. Bust. R. Ship. ½ penny, 1793. Bronze proof.
12 Belgium. Leopold I, II. Busts jugata. R. Bavaria, palace of Justice, etc. 5 Fr. in copper on semi-centl. of adoption of Const., 1830–80. Uncirculated.
13 Belgium. Lion seated. Pattern 20 cent, 1859. Nickel. Fine.
14 Belgium. Lion rampant. Pattern 20 cent, 1860. Nickel. Proofs. Diff. 3 pcs.
15 Belgium. Leopold I. Head. 20 cent, 1860. Nickel. Brilliant.
16 Brazil. Pedro II. 80 reis. Uncirculated. Large.
17 Buena Vista and Urachiche. ½, 1 real, 1858–68. Ranch tokens. Fine. 2 pcs.
18 Canada. Montreal and Lachine R. R. 3d Class Check. Fine. Rare.
19 Canada. Le Roux, Nos. 25, 28, 29, 30, 36, 44, 51, 55, 57, 62, (1758) 78, 79, 80, 82, 100 (1857), 105 (1882), 127, 133, 149, 162, 191, 196, 201, 209, 220, 223, 227. Fine to uncirculated. Choice lot. 27 pcs.
20 Caracas. Lion and shield. 1817–8. Fine. 2 pcs.
21 Carthagena. Indian, house and tree. 2 reales. Rude.
22 Catalonia. Isabella II. 3 quartos, 1837. Fine.
23 Cayenne. C crowned, fleur-de-lis crowned. V. g. 3 pcs.
24 Costa Rica. Arms. Centavo, 1865. Nickel. Very good.
25 Cyprus. Victor Amadeus II. Initials crowned. 1688. Fine.
26 Berg and Cleve. T Crowned. 3 Stuber, 1806. Very fine.

27 Dominica. Constitution and Cross. 2½, 5 centavos, 1877.
    Nickel. V. fine.   2 pcs.
28 England. Chas. I. Crown and sceptre. Farthing. Fine.
29 England. Wm. and Mary, Chas. II, Geo. I, II, III, IV,
    Victoria. Farthings. V. g. to uncirculated.   8 pcs.
30 England. Chas. II. St. Michael and dragon, etc. Pattern
    ½ penny. Brass. Poor but rare.
31 England. Geo. III. Bust. 2 pence, 1797. Large. V. good.
32 England. Victoria. Head. ⅓ farthing, 1866. Very good.
33 England. Male slave. AM I NOT A BROTHER. ½ penny. V.f.
34 France. Early tournois of 1590 to 1696. Good. Diff. 8 pcs.
35 France. Louis XVI. Young head. A beautiful coin of 1789.
36 France. Repub. 1793. Sphinx supplying a fountain from
    her breasts. 5 decimes. Uncirculated. Curious.
37 France. Nap. III. Satirical tokens. 2 Proofs, 1 v.g. Diff. 3 pcs.
38 Greece. George I. Head. 1, 5, 10 para. Bright red. 3 pcs.
39 Gibraltar. 1810, 1820, 1842. Very good.   3 pcs.
40 Guatemala. Range of volcanoes. Centavo, 1871. Uncir.
41 Guinea, French. Louis Philippe. 10 cent, 1846. Base. Fine.
42 Holland. Rampant lion. R. Lib. cap and shields. Token,
    1671. Bronzed. Very fine.
43 Honduras. Jamaica. Venezuela. Peru. Nickel. V. g. 7 pcs.
44 Ireland. Chas II. Jas II. ½ pennies and gun money shilling,
    1689. Fair and good.   3 pcs.
45 Ireland. Jas II. Bust. Gun money ½ crown, Aug. 1689. V. f.
46 Ireland. Jas II. Bust. Gun money ½ crown, Sept. 1689. Fine.
47 Ireland. Jas II. Bust. Gun money ½ crown, Oct. 1689. Fine.
48 Ireland. James II. Bust. Gun money ½ crown, May, 1690.
    Extremely fine.
49 Ireland. Dublin. Mic Wilson's ½ penny, (1672). Weak imp.
50 Isle of Man. Derby crest. R Trinacria. Penny, 1733. Ex-
    tremely fine. Rare.
51 Isle of Man. D A crowned (Duke of Athol.) R. Trinacria.
    ½ penny, 1758. Uncirculated. Rare.
52 Isle of Man. Geo. III. Bust. R. Trinacria. Penny, 1786. Fine.
53 Isle of Man. Same device. Fine. ½ penny, 1786. Fine.
54 Isle of Man. Trinacria. ½ penny, 1831. Very fine.
55 Indian or Persian dumps. 1 square, 1 round. Thick. 2 pcs.
56 Italy. Early Papal, etc. Rare siege piece. Good. 22 pcs.
57 Jersey. 2/13 of a shill. 1844. Essequebo, Stiver, 1813. V.f. 2 pcs.
58 Malta. Antoine Manoal de Villhena. Winged hand holding
    sword. R. Maltese cross. 1726. Fine. Rare.

59 Malta. Em De Rohan. Arms. 1780. V. g. 2 pcs.
60 Malacca. Rooster. Kepeng. Very fine.
61 Mentz. Fasces. Siege coin of 2 sols. 1793. Good.
62 Mexico. Yucatan. ½ grano, 1860. Lead. Rude. V. rare.
63 Mexico. Chihuahua, Indian. 1846–55. Good. 2 pcs.
64 Mexico. Zacatecas. Cupid. R. Monument, Octavo, 1829. Brass. Very fine.
65 Mysore. Elephant l. Very good.
66 New Granada. Liberty cap. 1 decimo, 1847. Very good.
67 Neuchatel. Alexander. 1 batz, 1809. Very good. Scarce.
68 Paraguay. Lion. ₁⁄₁₂ real, 1845. Cleaned. V.g. Scarce.
69 Paraguay. Star. 2, 4 Centesimos, 1870. Fine. 2 pcs.
70 Philippine Is. Ferd. VII. Arms. R. Lion. Quarto, 1830. Fine.
71 Roman Repub. Eagle on fasces. 4, 8 (silvered), ½, 3 Baiocchi. Very good. 4 pcs.
72 Russia. Alex. I. Eagle within circles. 5 Kop., 1804. Very good. Large.
73 Sandwich Is. Kamehameha III. Bust. Cent, 1847. V. f.
74 Santa Marta. ¼ real. 1820. Rude but very fine.
75 Sarawak. J. Brooke. Head. ¼ cent, 1863. Very fine.
76 St. Domingo. F 7 crowned. R. s. D. 1. Rude. Very good.
77 Scotland. Charles II. Farthing. Good.
78 Scotland. Charles II. Bust. R. Thistle. ½ p. 1678. Good.
79 Servia. Michael III. Head. 1, 5, 10 para, 1868. Uncirculated. Rare. 3 pcs.
80 Siam. Maha Monghut, 1851–68. Elephant. R Pagoda. ½ (copper), ⅛ (zinc) fuang. Very fine. 2 pcs.
81 Siam. 1874. ¼ fuang. Very fine.
82 Siberia. Cath. II. Sables and shield. 2 Kopecks, 1767. Very good.
83 Surinam. Coffee plant. 1764. Very fine. Scarce.
84 Sumatra. Arms. Kepeng, 1804. Very fine.
85 Sweden. Baron Gortz dalers. 1715–19, including last issue, i.e., with head. Fine to uncir. Extra fine set. 11 pcs
86 Tarracona. Isabella II. Proclamation piece, Dec., 1833. Good.
87 Tasmania. Kangaroo and Ostrich. Penny token of Lewis Abrahams, 1855. Uncirculated.
88 Tuscany. Provisional Gov't. 1, 2. 5 cent, 1859. Fine. 3 pcs.
89 U. S. 1837 Tokens. Contains several scarce varieties; viz. Head of Liberty l, surrounded by stars (2 var.), big-bellied donkey, Loco Foco, etc. V. g. to uncir. Different. 40 pcs.

90   Venice. 2 early coins. Very good.   2 pcs.
91   Venice. Provisional Gov't. 1, 3, 5 cent, 1849. Fine. 3 pcs.
92   Various countries. Balance of the collection. V. g. to fine.
     Desirable lot, selected by Mr. Collier "from 20,000 pieces."
                                                  270 pcs.
93   Jetons, old weights, etc. 2 pierced. V. g. to v. f. Diff. 30 pcs.
94   Rebellion Tokens. Different. Choice lot.   431 pcs.

FOREIGN SILVER COINS.

95   1458–94 Ferdinand I. Bust r., crowned, ins. trs., "Crowned
     because he strove legally." R. Crutch-cross and titles; trs.,
     "Ferdinand, by the Grace of God, King of Sicily, Jerusa-
     lem, Hungary." Struck on his coronation. Testoon. Ex-
     tremely fine.
96   1780 Hungary. Maria Theresa. Fine bust. Crown. Ex-
     tremely fine.
97   1807 Lucca and Piombino. Busts jugata of Felix Baciocchi
     and Eliza Bonaparte. Franc. Very fine.
98   1810 Spain. Joseph Napoleon. Bust. Dollar. V. g. Rare.
99   1822 Mexico. Augustin. Small head and eagle. Doll. Gd.
100   1826 Peru. Half dollar. On Oath of Allegiance. Ex. fine.
101   1834 Cuba. Isabella II. Proclamation real, 8 Feb., 1834.
     Pierced. Fine. Rare.
102   1836 Argentine Confed. Sun. R. Arms. Dollar. V. fine.
103   1840 Bolivia. Potosi. President Velasco. Bust. R. Justice.
     Sueldo. Very fine. Rare.
104   1849 Roman Republic. Wolf and twins. Set of siege coins
     for 5, 10, 20, 40 baiocchi. Diamond shape. Base silver.
     Uncirculated. Extremely rare. Sold for $11.40 in Warner
     sale.   4 pcs.
105   1856 Tuscany. Leopold II. Head. R. Florentine lily.
     Florin. Uncirculated.
106   1879 Austria. Franz Jos. I and Elizabeth. Beautiful heads
     jugata. Splendid double guilden on their silver wedding.
     Brilliant.
107   1883 Sandwich Is. Kalakaua I. Head. Dollar. Uncirculated.
108   Guatemala, Norway, India, Brunswick, Hungary, etc. Face,
     about 40 cts. each. V. gd. to uncir. Diff. Nice lot. 12 pcs.
109   Various countries. Very good. Diff. 20 cent size. 18 pcs.
110   Greece, Sicily, Poland 1831; early Russian, Malta 1723, etc.
     Very good to uncirculated. Dime size. Different. 20 pcs.

111 Russia (early), Ionian Is., Bolivia, Peru. Desirable lot. Very
good to uncirculated. Half-Dime size. Different. 45 pes.
112 Venice. Swiss. Different. Base. Very good to fine. 58 pes.
113 Bracteates. Strasburg. Good. 94 pes.
114 Bracteates. Mayence. Bishops of Bavarian House. 94 pes.

ENGLISH GOLD AND SILVER COINS.

115 Aethelred II, 978–1016. Bust l. R. Cross. Penny. Very fine.
116 William the Conqueror, 1066–87. Bust facing. R. Cross,
PAXS in angles. Penny. Very fine.
117 Richard I, 1189–99. Cross. R. Inscription in 3 lines. Poie-
tou penny. Fine.
118 Henry. Bust facing. Groat struck at London. Good.
119 Edward VI, 1547–53. Bust in ermine. Shilling. Very gd.
120 Elizabeth. Bust l., good portrait. Sixpence, 1573. Fine.
121 Commonwealth. St. George's cross on shield, within palm
and olive branch; THE COMMONWEALTH OF ENGLAND. R.
St. George's and Irish shields joined; GOD WITH US. Sover-
eign, 1651. Very fine. Slightly bent. Rare.
122 Charles II, George II, III, etc. Maundy money. Different.
2 pierced. Very good. 11 pes.
123 George III. Bust. Bank of England dollar, 1804. Fine.
124 Tokens. Northumberland, Stafford (pierced), Bank 5, 10,
18 pence. Very good. 7 pes.
125 Scotland. James III, 1460–88. Billon plac. Fair.
126 Scotland. Robert II, 1371–90. Bust l. Edinburgh groat.
Very fine. Rare.
127 Scotland. Robert II. Same device. Perth groat. Fine. Rare.

ENGLISH COPPER TOKENS.

128 Birmingham Workhouse 2/6, 1788. Beggar receiving alms
from a female. w counterstamped on obv. and rev. Brass.
Very fine. Rare.
129 Pennies. 2 very good, balance uncirculated. Diff. 9 pes.
130 Half-pennies. Contains 9 Revolutionary, Lady Godiva
1792, 3, 4, bright red, and others scarce. A splendid collection formed by Mr. Collier with much care and considerable
expense. 15 proofs, 55 uncirculated, 50 very fine, 46 fine,
55 very good, 27 good, 11 poor. Different and a desirable
lot. 259 pes.
131 Farthings. Bristol 1652, 62, 70. Norwich 1667. Gd. 4 pcs.
132 Farthings. 3 uncir., 6 very fine, 13 good. Different. 22 pcs.

ANCIENT GREEK SILVER COINS.

133 Aegina. B. C. 600. Tortoise. R. punch-mark. Obolus. Good.

134 Aegina. B. C. 560. Similar. Hemidrachm. Very good.

135 Persia. Darius I. B. C. 521 to 485. King as an archer kneeling. R. punch-mark. Daric or siglos. Fair.

136 Thasos. B. C. 465–411. Satyr on knee, bearing nymph in his arms. R. Punch-mark of four divisions. Didrachm. Fine.

137 Syracuse. B. C. 485. Head of Arethusa surrounded by four dolphins; ΣΥΡΑΚΟΣΙΟΝ. R. Quadriga. Tetradrachm. Very good.

138 Same. B. C. 460–412. Head in large cap ornamented with band. R. Quadriga. Tetradrachm. Very good.

139 Rhegium. B. C. 500. Mask of lion. R. Demos seated; REGINON. Hemidrachm. Fine.

140 Ephesus. B. C. 400 to 336. Bee; E. Φ. R. Forepart of stag, to l. palm-tree;)ΗΣΤΑΝΑΞ(. Tetradrachm. Very rare. Fine, surface eroded.

141 Thurium. Finest Art. B. C. 400 to 345. Head of Pallas, on helmet Scylla. R. Bull trotting; ΘΟΥΡΙΩΝ. Didrachm. Very good.

142 Metapontum. B. C. 300. Head of Ares wearing Corinthian helmet. R. Wheat-ear, META. Didrachm. Fine.

143 Velia. B. C. 300 to 275. Head of Pallas l. R. Lion gnawing bone; (Υ)ΕΛΗΤΩ(Ν). Didrachm. Very good.

REGAL.

144 Alexander the Great. *Macedonia.* Head of Pallas r. R. Nike standing; ΑΛΕΞΑΝΔΡΟΥ. Stater, gold. Fine, solder mark on edge.

145 Same. Head of Herakles. R. Zeus seated; ΑΛΕΞΑΝΔΡΟΥ ΒΑΣΙΛΕΩΣ. Tetradrachm. Very good.

146 Alexander IV. Head of Alexander the Great with horn of Ammon, covered with elephant skin. R. Pallas (after archaic statue) hurling javelin to r.; ΑΛΕΞΑΝΔΡΟΥ, in field helmet, ΠΡ and eagle, the last the badge of Ptolemaeus, by whom this coin was struck whilst Governor in Egypt for the infant son of Alexander. Tetradrachm. Fine. V. rare.

147 Ptolemaeus I. *Egypt.* Head to r. R. Eagle; ΠΤΟΛΕΜΑΙΟΥ ΒΑΣΙΛΕΩΣ. Tetradrachm. Good.

148 Philip, last king of *Syria.* Head to r. R. Zeus seated; (ΒΑ) ΣΙΛΕ(ΛΩΣ) ΦΙΛΙΠΠΟ(Υ) ΕΠΙΦΑΝΟΥ(Σ) (ΦΙ)ΛΑΔΕΛ(ΦΟΥ). Tetradrachm. Fair.

COPPER COINS OF THE PTOLEMÆI.

149 Ptolemaeus III. Euergetes. *Phœnicia.* Head of Zeus Ammon r. R. Eagle; ΠΤΟΛΕΜΑΙΟΥ ΒΑΣΙΛΕΩΣ, in field cornucopiæ. Fine. Size 26.

150 Ptolemaeus IV. Similar, but R. cornucopiæ on eagle's l. shoulder. Fine. 24.

151 Ptolemaeus V. Epiphanes. Similar. R. without symbol; mon. between eagle's legs. Fine.

152 Ptolemaeus VIII. Head of Cleopatra I r. as Isis with long curls. R. as above. Fine. Rare. 17.

153 Various. Large and small. Poor.   8 pieces.

154 ROMA. Tiberius. Aureus. Head r. TI CAESAR DIVI AVG F AVGVSTVS. R. Livia seated; PONTIF MAXIM. Very fine.

AMERICAN COLONIAL AND STATE COINS.

155 1652 Mass. Pine-tree shilling. Very good. Rare.

156 1652 Mass. Pine-tree shilling. Clipped close on upper edge. Good. Rare.

157 (1681) N. J. Mark Newby farthing. Issue in America authorized in 1681. Fine.

158 1722 Wood ½ penny. Harp before figure. Fine. Scarce thus.

159 1722 Louisiana. L's crowned. Very good.

160 1722 Rosa Americana. Geo. I. Head. R. Full-blown rose. 2 pence. Very good. Rare.

161 1722 Rosa Americana. Same device. Penny. Good.

162 1723 Rosa Americana. Obv. as last. R. Crowned rose. ½, 1, 2 pence. V. g. Rare set.   3 pcs.

163 1773 Virginia. Geo. III. Bust. ½ penny. Very good.

164 1783 Nova Constellatio. Radiated eye. R. U. S, in wreath; LIBERTAS JUSTITIA 1783. Very fine.

165 1783 Nova Constellatio. Eye in double set of rays. V. g.

166 1785 Nova Constellatio. Eye in small rays. R. U. S. in script. Fine.

167 1785 Vermont. Range of hills and plow, VERMONTIS RES PUBLICA. Good. Rare.

168 1786 Vermont. Same device. 7 trees on mountains, VERMONTENSIUM. Fair.

169 1786 Vermont. Same device. 9 trees. Fine. Light olive.

170 1786 Vermont. Young head r. "Baby Head." AUCTORI VERMON. R. Liberty l; INDE ET LIB. Fine. One of the best we have seen of this rare piece. C, 1-c.

171   1787 Vermont. Similar to last. Very good. C, 1-A.
172   1787 Vermont. Similar obv. R. BRITANNIA (faint). Good.
173   1785 Conn. Bust r. "Negro head," AUCTORI CONNEC. Head f.
174   1785 Conn. Fine. Light brown color. C, 6-G, rarity 4.
175   1786 Conn. Mailed bust l. C, 5-G, rarity 6, another 5-H. 2 pcs.
176   1787 Conn. Small head, large shoulders. R. ET LIB INDE.
        Good. Rare. C, 1-A.
177   1787 Conn. Large head, called "Gov Bradford." Weak impression as all are, but one of the best we have seen. C, 1-c, rarity 4.
178   1787 Conn. "Horned bust." V. g. C, 4-L.
179   1787 Conn. V. f. Even impression. C, 12-Q, rarity 5.
180   1787 Conn. Fine. C, 13-D, rarity 4.
181   1787 Conn. Very good. C, 20-A, rarity 4.
182   1787 Conn. Very good. C, 33-T, rarity 5.
183   1787 Conn. Very good. C, 37-K.
184   1787 Conn. AUCTOPI ET II B. Very good. C, 41-I.
185   1787 Conn. CONNFC. Very good. C, 43-Y, rarity 4.
186   1788 Conn. Bust with small head and large shoulders same as No. 1, 1787, rev. same as Vermont, 1788, rev. B. See Crosby, Plate V, obv. No. 11, rev. of No. 4, also see note p. 218, where he says it is *unique*. This specimen is rather weakly struck on rev., the date is off, but the obv. is very good. Weight 100 grs.
187   1788 Conn. Bust r. C, 2-D*, rarity 3. Fine.
188   1788 Conn. Bust l. Fine. C, 11-G, rarity 3.
189   1787 N. Y. Bust r., NOVA EBORAC. R. Lib. to l. Good.
190   1787 N. Y. IMMUNIS COLUMBIA. Poor, but rare.
191   1787 N. J. Horse head and plow. Good. M, 6-D.
192   1787 N. J. Plow with straight beam. V. f. M, 52-i.
193   1787 N. J. Horse with long crooked neck. V. g. M, 54-K.
194   1787 N. J. Large horse head. Good. M, 63-s.
195   1788 N. J. Horse head and plow to l. Gd. Rare. M, 50-f.
196   1788 N. J. Horse head r. R. Small horse at end of legend. Very fine, and one of the best we have seen. Rare. M, 75-bb.
197   1788 N. J. Same variety. Fair.
198   1788 N. J. Variety, but with horse on rev. V. g. Rare. M, 78-dd.
199   1787 Mass. Indian standing. Cent. Good.
200   1788 Mass. Same device. Cent. Fine.
201   1787 U. S. Sun-dial. FUGIO. Fine.
202   (1791) Ky. Cent. Thin planchet. Good.
203   1778-9 Rhode Is. Medal or token. Fair.

204 1783 Washington cent. Double head. Very good.
205 1783 Washington. GEORGIUS TRIUMPHO. Very good.
206 (1795) Washington. Bust l. LIBERTY AND SECURITY. Ex. f.
207 1794 N. Y. Talbot, Allum and Lee. Very good.
208 1795 N. Y. Similar. Fine.
209 Bar cent, Bolen's copy. Ky. cent, elect.   2 pcs.

FIRST U. S. GOLD COIN.

210 1795 Eagle. Beautiful head of Liberty. R. Eagle with olive
     wreath in beak, standing on a palm branch. V. fine. Rare.

DOLLARS.

211 1795 Head. Very fine. Sharp stars.
212 1795 Bust. Very good.
213 1796 Large date, small letters on rev. Very fine. Scarce.
214 1796 Small date, large letters on rev. Very fine. Scarce.
215 1797 6 stars facing. Very fine. Dent on forehead. Scarce.
216 1797 7 stars facing. Fine. Scarce.
217 1798 13 stars. R. Small eagle. Very fine. Bold even im-
     pression. Rare.
218 1798 13 stars. R. Heraldic eagle. Fine.
219 1799 over 1798. Weak impression. Very slightly rubbed.
220 1799 5 stars facing. Very good. Rare.
221 1799 6 stars facing. Extremely fine, showing but the faintest
     touch of cabinet friction. Lustre.
222 1800 Extremely fine. Faint dent on chin. Lustre. Beautiful.
223 1801 Very good. Scarce.
224 1802 Extremely fine.
225 1803 Large 3. Very fine.
226 1803 Small 3. Extremely fine. Lustre. A rare coin which
     is very seldom offered.
227 1840 Very fine. Scarce.
228 1841 Extremely fine. Slight proof-surface. Scarce.
229 1842 Very fine.
230 1845 Good. Dent on edge. Very scarce.
231 1847 Very fine.
232 1849 Fine.
233 1850 Very good. O mint.
234 1853 Very fine.
235 1855 Very fine. Faint dent on rim. Rare.
236 1859 Uncirculated. O mint.
237 1861 Uncirculated.

238   1863 Has been a proof. Very fine. Scarce.
239   1864 Good. Scarce.
240   1865 Very good. Scarce.
241   1866 Extremely fine. 1st year with motto.
242   1869 Brilliant proof.
243   1873 Standard. Has been a proof. Very fine.
244   1873 Trade. Proof. Scarce.
245   1876 Trade. Uncirculated.
246   1877 Trade. San Francisco mint. Uncirculated.
247   1877 Trade. Brilliant proof.
248   1878 Trade. Brilliant proof.
249   1878 Standard. 8 feathers in eagle's tail. Proof.
250a   1879 Trade. Brilliant proof.
250   1880 Trade. Brilliant proof.

HALF DOLLARS.

251   1794 Very good. Strong impression. Rare.
252   1794 Very good. Slight variety. Rare.
253   1795 "Small head," the hair is shorter than in the ordinary
     variety. Very good, and one of the best we have seen.
254   1795 Head with long flowing locks. Fine.
255   1795 Variety, curl passes through the last star. Very good.
256   1795 Variety, curl touches two points of last star. Very
     good.
257   1795 Variety, curl far from star. Very good.
258   1795 Variety, curl between points of last star. Very good.
259   1795 Variety. *Three leaves* under eagle's wing. Poor. Rare.
260   1796 16 stars. Very good. An excellent specimen of this
     excessively rare coin.
261   1797 Very good. Also an excellent specimen. Excessively
     rare.
262   1801 Fine. Rare.
263   1802 Fine. Rare.
264   1803 Large 3. Very fine. Sharp.
265   1803 Small 3. Good. Scarce.
266   1805 over 1804. Stars behind head weak. Very fine. Rare.
267   1805 5 berries on laurel. Very fine.
268   1806 Pointed 6. Over 1800? Cracked die. Scratch from edge
     to ear. Fine.
269   1806 Pointed 6. Faint nick near eye. Uncirculated. Bril-
     liant mint lustre.

270 1806 Pointed 6. Stem of branch does not pass through claw.
    Very fine.
271 1806 (blunt 6) over 1805. Very good. Very rare.
272 1806 Blunt 6. Close date. Fine.
273 1806 Blunt 6. Wide date. Very fine.
274 1807 Bust to r. Fine.
275 1807 Bust to l. Uncirculated. Sharp, beautiful specimen
    with mint lustre. Scarce.
276 1808 over 1807. Extremely fine.
277 1808 Extremely fine. Weak impression.
278 1809 Extremely fine.
279 1810 Uncirculated. Even impression.
280 1811 Uncirculated. Sharp, beautiful impression with mint
    lustre.
281 1811 Wide and separated dates. Very good.   2 pcs.
282 1812 Uncirculated. Brilliant mint lustre.
283 1813 Fine.
284 1814 over 1813. Uncirculated. Sharp, beautiful impression
    with mint lustre. Scarce.
285 1814 Perfect date. Very fine. Drift marks across head.
286 1815 Fine. Rare.
287 1817 over 1813. Very good. Scarce.
288 1817 Wide date. Very fine.
289 1818 over 1817. Uncirculated. Sharp.
290 1818 Perfect date. Uncirculated. Sharp.
291 1818 Date thus, 1 81 8. Extremely fine.
292 1818 Wide date. Very fine. Nick under ear.
293 1819 over 1818. Very fine.
294 1819 Perfect date. Extremely fine. E H scratched on R.
295 1820 over 1819. Extremely fine. Scarce.
296 1820 Perfect date. Extremely fine.
297 1821 Fine.
298 1822 Extremely fine.
299 1822 Variety. Fine.
300 1823 Uncirculated. Mint lustre.
301 1823 Extremely fine. Double profile.
302 1823 Extremely fine.
303 1824 over 1821. Fine.
304 1824 Perfect date. Very fine.
305 1825 Very fine.
306 1826 Varieties. Very fine.   3 pcs.
307 1827 Curled 2. Fine. Very scarce.

308 1827 Figure 2 with straight base. Very good.
309 1828 Large curled 2. Uncirculated. Lustre. Scarce.
310 1828 Curled 2 with knob. Very fine. Scarce.
311 1828 Figure 2 with straight base. Uncirculated. Sharp.
312 1828 Small 8. Extremely fine.
313 1829 over 1821? Uncirculated.
314 1829 Perfect date. Fine.
315 1830 Large and small 0 in date. Very fine.   2 pcs.
316 1831 Very fine.
317 1832 Uncirculated. Sharp.
318 1832 Uncirculated.
319 1833 Uncirculated. Mint lustre.
320 1834 Small date and letters. Uncirculated.
321 1834 Large date, small letters. Uncirculated.
322 1834 Large date, large letters. Uncirculated.
323 1835 Uncirculated. Lustre.
324 1836 Very fine.
325 1836 Gobrecht head. Milled edge. Three scratches from
      mouth to edge. Fine. Rare.
326 1837 Very fine.
327 1838 Uncirculated.
328 1839 Bust of Liberty. Very fine.
329 1839 Bust of Liberty; O (N. Orleans) over date. Very fine.
330 1839 Liberty seated with and without drapery from elbow.
      Fine.   2 pcs.
331 1840 Reverse of 1839 (Bust). Very good. Rare.
332 1840 Uncirculated.
334 1840 Extremely fine. Lustre. N. Orleans mint.
335 1841 Extremely fine.
336 1841 Very fine. New Orleans mint.
337 1842 Small date. Uncirculated.
338 1842 Small date. Very good. O. mint. Mr. Collier states this
      has never before been offered in a sale.
339 1842 Large date. Uncirculated.
340 1842 O. mint. Large date. Very good.
341 1843 Very fine.
342 1844 Extremely fine.   .
343 1844 Very fine.
344 1844 O. mint. Fine.
345 1845 Extremely fine.
346 1845 O. mint. Very fine.
347 1846 over 1845? Extremely fine. Very rare.

348   1846 O. mint. Small date. Uncirculated.
349   1846 Large date. Uncirculated.
350   1846 O. mint. Large date. Fine.
351   1847 Uncirculated.
352   1847 O. Mint. Uncir., proof surface. Rare in this state.
353   1848 Uncirculated.
354   1848 O. mint. Uncirculated.
355   1849 Uncirculated.
356   1849 O. mint. Uncirculated.
357   1850 Uncirculated.
358   1850 O. mint. Very fine.
359   1851 Very fine. Scarce.
360   1851 O. Mint. Very fine. Scarce.
361   1851 O. mint. Variety. Very fine. Scarce.
362   1852 Uncirculated. Rare.
363   1852 O. mint. Good. Rare.
364   1853 Very fine. Only year with arrow heads and rays.
365   1853 O. mint. Very fine.
366   1854 O. mint. Very fine.
367   1854 O. mint. Variety. Uncirculated.
368   1855 O. mint. Extremely fine.
369   1855 San Francisco mint. Good. Very rare.
370   1856 Uncirculated.
371   1856 O. mint. Uncirculated.
372   1856 San Francisco mint. Very good. Rare.
373   1857 Philadelphia and Orleans. Fine. 1854 very fine. 3 pcs.
374   1857 San Francisco mint. Good. Rare.
375   1858 Brilliant proof. Rare.
376   1858 O. mint. Uncirculated,
377   1858 San Francisco mint, small s. Uncirculated. Rare.
378   1858 San Francisco mint, large s. Fine. Rare.
379   1859 Very fine.
380   1859 O. mint. Extremely fine.
381   1859 San Francisco mint. Poor.
382   1860 Uncirculated.
383   1860 O. mint. Extremely fine.
384   1860 San Francisco mint. Very fine. Scarce.
385   1861 Uncirculated.
386   1861 O. mint. Uncirculated. Faint nicks.
387   1861 San Francisco mint, small s. Extremely fine. Rare.
388   1861 San Francisco mint, large s. Extremely fine. Rare.
389   1862 Brilliant proof.

390 1862 San Francisco mint. Fine.
391 1863 Uncirculated.
392 1863 San Francisco mint. Very good. Scarce.
393 1864 Brilliant proof. Rare.
394 1864 San Francisco mint, large s. Extremely fine. Rare.
395 1864 San Francisco mint, small s. Very good. Rare.
396 1865 Uncirculated.
397 1865 San Francisco mint. Fine. Rare.
398 1866 Uncirculated. First year of IN GOD WE TRUST.
399 1866 San Francisco mint. With motto. Uncirculated.
400 1867 Uncirculated.
401 1868 Uncirculated.
402 1868 San Francisco mint. Very good.
403 1869 Very fine.
404 1869 San Francisco mint. Very good.
405 1870 Extremely fine.
406 1871 Very fine.
407 1871 San Francisco mint. Uncirculated.
408 1871 Carson City mint. Good.
409 1872 Very fine.
410 1873 Without arrows. Very fine.
411 1873 San Francisco mint. With arrows. Fine.
412 1873 Carson City mint. With arrows. Uncir.
413 1874 Carson City mint. Very fine.
414 1875 San Francisco mint. Uncirculated.
415 1876 San Francisco mint. Extremely fine.
416 1877 San Francisco and P. mints. Uncir.   2 pcs.
417 1878 Extremely fine.
418 1879 Uncirculated.
419 1879 $\frac{1}{2}$, $\frac{1}{4}$, $\frac{1}{10}$. Uncirculated.   3 pcs.
420 1879 Duplicate sets. Uncirculated.   6 pcs.
421 1880 Uncirculated. Proof surface.
422 1881 Uncirculated. Scarce.
423 1882 Uncirculated. Scarce.
424 1883 Uncirculated. Scarce.
425 1884 Uncirculated. Scarce.
426 1884 $\frac{1}{2}$, $\frac{1}{4}$, $\frac{1}{10}$. Very fine.   3 pcs.
427 1885 Brilliant proof. Scarce.
428 1885 Uncirculated. Scarce.
429 1885 $\frac{1}{2}$, $\frac{1}{4}$, $\frac{1}{10}$. Uncirculated. Scarce.   3 pcs.
430 1885 Duplicate set. Same condition.   3 pcs.

QUARTER DOLLARS.

431 1796 Good. Rare.
432 1804 Very good. Superior to those usually offered. Strong impression. Rare.
433 1805 Fine. Seldom seen better.
434 1805 Very good. Scratched on reverse.
435 1806 over 1805. Very good. Scarce.
436 1806 Very fine. Bold impression. Rare.
437 1806 Variety. Good.
438 1807 Small date. Fine. Bent at left of date.
439 1807 Large date. Fair.
440 1815 Uncirculated. E lightly stamped above head. Sharp.
441 1818 Very fine.
442 1818 Variety, date very wide. Very good.
443 1819 Small date. Fine. Scarce.
444 1819 Large date. Good.
445 1820 Fine.
446 1821 Very good.
447 1822 Good. Scarce.
448 1824 Very good. Rare.
449 1825 over 1821 ? Fine.
450 1825 Very good.
451 1828 Fine.
452 1828 Slight variety. Very good.
453 1831 Uncirculated. Large letters on rev.
454 1831 Very fine. Small letters on rev.
455 1832 Very fine.
456 1833 Very fine.
457 1834 Uncirculated.
458 1834 Varieties. Fine.   2 pcs.
459 1835 Extremely fine. Nick on neck.
460 1836 Fine.
461 1837 Very fine.
462 1838 Bust of Liberty. Very fine.
463 1838 Liberty seated. Very fine. Weak impression.
464 1839 Fine.
465 1840 O mint. Without drapery from elbow to knee. Very good.
466 1840 With drapery from elbow to knee. Very good. Scarce.
467 1841 Fine.
468 1842 O mint. Very fine.

3

469   1843 Uncirculated.
470   1843 O mint. Very good.
471   1844 Very fine.
472   1845 Fine.
473   1846-7 Good.   2 pcs.
474   1848 Fine.
475   1849 Very good.
476   1850 P. & O. 1851 O. 1852 O. 1857 O. Good.   5 pcs.
477   1851 Uncirculated. Scarce.
478   1852 Extremely fine. Scarce.
479   1853 Arrow heads and rays, only year of this type. Very
      fine.
480   1854 Uncirculated.
481   1855 Very fine. Scarce.
482   1855 San Francisco mint. Good. Rare.
483   1856 Uncirculated.
484   1856 Very fine.
485   1857 Uncirculated.
486   1857, 8, 9, 60, 4, 5, 9, 71. San Francisco mint. Fair. 8 pcs.
487   1858 Extremely fine.
488   1860 Uncirculated.
489   1860 (O) 61, 2, 72, 73 no arrows. Fine.   5 pcs.
490   1862 Uncirculated.
491   1863 Uncirculated.
492   1864 Uncirculated.
493   1865 Uncirculated.
494   1866 Uncirculated.
495   1867 Uncirculated.
496   1868 Uncirculated.
497   1869 Uncirculated.
498   1870 Proof.
499   1871 Proof.
500   1872 Uncirculated.
501   1873 Arrows. Uncirculated.
502   1874, 5, 6, 7 (2). San Francisco. Uncirculated.   5 pieces.
503   1875, 6, 7, 8, 9, 80. Uncirculated.   6 pieces.
504   1879 Uncirculated.
505   1880 Uncirculated.
506   1881 Uncirculated.
507   1882 Uncirculated.
508   1885 Uncirculated.

TWENTY CENT PIECES.

509   1875 San Francisco.   Uncirculated.
510   1876 Proof. Scarce.
511   1876 Uncirculated.   Mint lustre.   Scarce.
512   1877 Brilliant proof.   Rare.
513   1878 Brilliant proof.   Rare.

DIMES.

514   1796 Very good.   Rare.
515   1797 13 stars.   Very fine.   Strong even impression.   We know
         of only one specimen to equal and not any to surpass it.
         Excessively rare and valuable.
516   1798 Perfect date.   Fine.   Very rare.
517   1798 over 1797.   Good.   Very rare.
518   1802 Poor, date very good.   Very rare.
519   1803 Poor, date very good.   Rare.
520   1804 Fine for date.   Excessively rare; being fully equal to
         the 1823 quarter dollar.
521   1805 Uncirculated.   A few very faint drift marks on obv.
         Sharp beautiful impression with mint lustre.   Rare thus.
522   1807 Very good.
523   1809 Good.   Rare.
524   1811 over 1809.   Fine.   Rare.
525   1814 Small date.   Fine.
526   1814 Large date.   Fine.
527   1820 Very good.
528   1821 Small date.   Very fine.
529   1821 Large date.   Very fine.
530   1822 Very good.   Small L stamped over head.   Rare.
531   1823–4 Poor.   2 pcs.
532   1824 over 1822.   Uncirculated.   Sharp stars.   Mint lustre.
         Extremely rare in this condition.
533   1825 Fine.
534   1827 Very fine.
535   1828 Small date, very good.   Large date, poor.   2 pcs.
536   1829 Fine.
537   1831 Uncirculated.
538   1832 Uncirculated.
539   1832 Extremely fine.
540   1833 Uncirculated.
541   1833 Uncirculated.
542   1834 Uncirculated.

543   1835 Uncirculated.
544   1835 Uncirculated.
545   1836 Very fine.
546   1836 Very fine.
547   1837 Bust. Extremely fine.
548   1837 Liberty seated. Large curved date. Very fine.
549   1838 New Orleans mint. Without stars. Uncirculated. Sharp
         impression with mint lustre. Excessively rare in this
         condition.
550   1838 Same. Very good.
551   1838 With stars. Uncirculated.
552   1839 Extremely fine.
553   1840 With drapery from elbow to knee. Very good.
554   1840 Without drapery. Uncirculated.
555   1841 Orleans mint. Very fine.
556   1842 Very fine.
557   1844 Very good. Scarce.
558   1846 Very good. Dents in field. Scarce.
559   1850 Uncirculated.
560   1851 Uncirculated. Scarce.
561   1852 Uncirculated. Scarce.
562   1852 Very fine.
563   1852 Orleans mint. Very fine.
564   1853 Without arrows. Very good. Scarce.
565   1853 Without arrows (2), 4, 6. Very fine.   4 pieces.
566   1856 Large date. Very good. Scarce.
567   1858 San Francisco mint. Poor. Mr. Collier states that this
         is the only specimen he knows of, and that it is a rarity.
568   1859 Proof.
569   1860 Uncirculated.
570   1860 Stars on obv. San Francisco mint. Fair.
571   1863 Proof.
572   1864 Proof.
573   1865 Proof.
574   1866 Proof.
575   1867 Proof.
576   1868 Proof.
577   1870 Proof.
578   1874 Proof.
579   1875 Proof.
580   1876 Proof.
581   1877 Proof.
582   1878 Proof.

583 1814 ld. 1820, 9, 30, 7, 8, 9, 40, 3, 45, 47, 62, 72, 73, 2 var., 74.
Good to v. g. Various mint marks. 39 pcs.

584 1859, 62, 4, 6, 7, 9, 70, 1, 3, 5, 6, 7. San Francisco mint.
Fair to uncir. 13 pcs.

585 1868, 9, 75, 8, 82, 4, 5. Uncir. 10 pcs.

586 1875 2 var. 6, 7, 8. Uncir. Carson City mint. 5 pcs.

HALF DIMES.

587 1795, 1800, 1803. V. poor. 5 pierced. 7 pcs.

588 1851 Orleans mint. Uncirculated.

589 1858 Proof. Rare.

590 1860 Orleans mint. UNITED STATES OF AMERICA on obv. R.
Wreath enclosing HALF DIME. Uncirculated.

591 1860 *with stars* on obv. in place of ins. R. same as last.
Uncirculated. Extremely rare.

592 1862 Uncirculated.

593 1870 Proof.

594 1873 Proof. Last year of issue.

595 1829, 32, 5 (l and s dates), 7 (2 types), 8, 40, 4, 50, 2, 8, 9, 60,
2, 9, 72. V. g. to uncir. 18 pcs.

THREE CENT SILVER.

596 1851 O. mint. Uncirculated. Mint lustre.

597 1851 Philadelphia mint. Same condition as last.

598 1852 Uncirculated.

599 1853 Uncirculated. Brilliant lustre.

600 1854 Uncirculated. Sharp impression.

601 1855 Uncirculated. Mint lustre. Rare.

602 1856 Very fine.

603 1857 Uncirculated. Mint lustre.

604 1858 Uncirculated. Sharp. Mint lustre.

605 1859 Proof.

606 1860 Proof.

607 1861 Very fine.

608 1862 Proof.

609 1863 Proof. Rare.

610 1864 Proof. Rare.

611 1865 Proof. Rare.

612 1866 Proof. Scarce.

613 1867 Proof. Scarce.

614 1868 Proof. Scarce.

615 1869 Proof. Scarce.

616   1870 Uncirculated.   Slight proof surface.
617   1871 Proof.
618   1872 Proof.
619   1873 Proof.   Last year of issue.   Rare.

CENTS.

620   1793 Chain.   AMERICA.   Fine.   Dark color.   Very rare.
621   1793 Wreath.   Edge lettered ONE HUNDRED FOR A DOLLAR.
        Very good.   Oxidized surface.   Dark color.   Rare.
622   1794 Very good.   Has been cleaned.   F, 2, 2d rev.
623   1794 Poor.   Obv. scratched, spots of corrosion on rev.   F 3.
624   1794 Uncirculated.   Surface eroded.   Dark brown color.
        Strong imp.   F 4 but a rev, differing from his.
625   1794 V. f.   Rather a faint impression.   Light olive.   F 5, 2d rev.
626   1794 Uncir.   Surface slightly oxidized.   Steel color.   F 7, 2d rev.
627   1794 Very fine.   Weak impression on latter half of LIBERTY.
        Light olive.   F 10.
628   1794 Very good.   Light brown color.   F 11, 2d rev.
629   1794 Fine.   Dark color.   F 16, 1st rev.
630   1794 Good.   F 20, 1st rev.
631   1794 Fine.   Steel color.   Edge on rev. slightly dented in
        three places.   F 20 rev. of No. 26.
632   1794 Good.   Same variety but obv. die cracked across.
632a 1794 Poor.   1 pierced.   5 pcs.
633   1795 Thick planchet lettered edge.   V. g.   Strong impression.
        Dark color.   Rare.
634   1795 Thin planchet.   ONE CENT high in wreath.   Very good.
635   1795 Thin planchet.   ONE CENT in centre of wreath.   V. good.
        Light color.   Scarce.
636   1796 Liberty cap.   Date distant from bust.   V. g.   Scarce.
637   1796 Bust.   Fair.
638   1797 Very good.
639   1798 over 1797.   Good.
640   1798 Small date.   Fine.   Dark color.
641   1799 Perfect date.   Strong even impression for the piece, the
        date remarkably fine, the 9's showing the knobs, the word
        LIBERTY strong, as is also every part of the reverse.   Unusu-
        ally fine for date.   Dark color.   One of the best cents of
        this year that we have seen.   Excessively rare.   Cost Mr.
        Collier $35, and well worth it.
642   1800 Erroneous die.   79 showing under 80.   Very good.
643   1800 Perfect date.   Hair delicately tooled.   Fine.

644 1801 $\frac{1}{000}$ on R. Die broken at point of bust. Very good. Dark color.

645 1801 $\frac{1}{000}$ only one stem extends below bow. UNITED spelled IINITED. Good. Rare.

646 1802 Without ends to stems of wreath. Very fine. Light olive. Rare.

647 1802 With ends to stems of wreath. Good.

648 1803 Small $\frac{1}{100}$. Very fine. Spot of corrosion on rev. which could probably be removed. Olive color.

649 1803 Without ends to stems of wreath. Fine. Rare.

650 1803 Double fraction line. Very good.

651 1803 Large $\frac{1}{100}$. Cracked die. Fine. Dark color.

652 1803 $\frac{1}{100}$ over $\frac{1}{000}$. Fair. Rare variety.

653 1804 Perfect date. Very fair. Very rare.

654 1805 Fine. Steel color. Scarce in this condition.

655 1805, 1806, 1816 perfect date. Poor.   3 pcs.

656 1806 Very fine. Strong impression. Dark steel color. Very rare thus.

657 1807 over 6. Fine. Dark olive.

658 1807 Perfect date. Fine. Nick in field. Dark brown color.

659 1807 Perfect die. Has been burnished.

660 1808 Fine. Small spots of corrosion adhering to rev. Dark brown color.

661 1809 Very good, date very sharp. Corroded surface. Rare.

662 1810 Perfect date. Very good.

663 1811 Perfect date. Very good indeed. Dark color. Rare.

664 1812 Small date. Very good.

665 1812 Large date. Very good. Cleaned red.

666 1813 Fine. R. Stained inside wreath. Scarce.

667 1813 Fine. Scarce.

668 1814 Plain 4. Very good.

669 1814 Crossed 4. Very fine. Dark color.

670 1816 Perfect die. Uncirculated. Steel color.

671 1816 Broken die. Uncirculated. Light olive.

672 1817 13 stars. Uncir. Beautiful cent of light olive color.

673 1817 13 stars. Extremely fine.

674 1817 15 stars. Very fine. Light color. Scarce.

675 1818 Perfect die. Very fine. Light olive.

676 1818 Broken die. Uncirculated. Bright red.

677 1819 Large date. Over 1818. Extremely fine. Light olive.

678 1819 Large date. Very fine. Brown color.

679 1819 Small date. Uncirculated. Partly red.

680   1820 over 1819. Very fine. Dark color.
681   1820 Broken die. Uncirculated. Light olive.
682   1821 Very good. Dark color. Scarce.   ,
683   1822 Good.
684   1823 over 1822. Fair. Scarce.
685   1823 Perfect date. Very good. Bold impression. Scarce.
686   1824 With inner line. Fine. Scarce in this condition.
687   1824 Without inner line. Very good.
688   1825 Fine. Dark olive.
689   1826 Fine. Dark olive.
690   1827 Very fine. Light olive.
691   1828 Large date. Uncirculated. Sharp even impression.
         Cleaned, now a red-purple color. Rare.
692   1828 Small date. Very fine. Light olive color slightly
         rubbed. Very rare in this condition.
693   1829 Fine. Bold impression. Light color.
694   1830 Fine. Dark olive.
695   1831 Very fine. Showing traces of red.
696   1832 Fine. Has been bronzed.
697   1833 Very fine. Light olive.
698   1834 Large date. Fine. Scarce.
699   1834 Small date. Very fine. Dark color.
700   1835 Small date. Uncirculated. Dark olive. Stars flat as
         usual. Deep even milling. Rare.
701   1835 Large date. Very fine. Strong impression, Rare.
702   1836 Perfect die. Very good. Light olive.
703   1836 Broken die. Very fine.
704   1837 Plain hair string. Very fine.
705   1837 Plain hair string. Cracked die. Very fine.
706   1837 Beaded hair string. Cracked die. Fine. Light olive.
707   1838 Very fine. Dark olive.
708   1839 over 1836. Poor, but very rare.
709   1839 1838 head. Fine.
710   1839 Booby head. Very fine.
711   1839 Silly head. Uncirculated. Splendid sharp even im-
         pression. Faint crack in die across head. Red turning to
         steel color. A beautiful cent. Rare.
712   1839 1840 head. Very fine. Brown color.
713   1840 Large date. Cracked die. Very good.
714   1840 Small date. Extremely fine. Red-brown color.
715   1840 Small date. Fine.
716   1841 Very fine. Light olive.

717   1842 Large date. Very fine. Light olive.
718   1842 Small date. Fine. Light brown color.
719   1843 1842 obv. and rev. Fine. Brown color.
720   1843 1842 obv. and 1844 rev. Fine. Brown color.
721   1843 1844 obv. and 1844 rev. Uncirculated. Traces of origi-
        nal red color. Rare.
722   1844 Uncirculated. Die cracked on rim. Steel color. Rare.
723   1845 Very fine.
724   1846 Small date. Uncirculated. Steel color.
725   1846 Large date. Very fine. Light olive. One of the best
        we have seen of this variety. Rare.
726   1847 Uncirculated. Traces of original color.
727   1848 Uncirculated. Dull-red color.
728   1849 Uncirculated. Light olive.
729   1850 Uncirculated. Cleaned red.
730   1851 Uncirculated. Partly red.
731   1851 Uncirculated. Handsome color.
732   1852 Uncirculated. Partly red.
733   1852 Uncirculated. Bright red.
734   1853 Uncirculated. Bright red.
735   1854 Uncirculated. Light olive.
736   1855 Upright 55. Uncirculated.
737   1855 Slanting 55. Uncirculated.
738   1855 Slanting 55. Very fine.
739   1856 Slanting and straight 55. Uncirculated.   2 pcs.
740   1857 Small date. Fine.
741   1857 Large date. Uncirculated. Partly red.
742   1793 very poor, date does not show. 94, 5, 7 (2), 8 (3), 1800,
        2, 3 (2), 5, 8 (2), 9 (2), 10 (2), 13 (2), 16 (2), 17 (4), 18 (3), 19
        (2), 20, 1 (3), 2 (5), 3, 4 (4), 5 (4), 6 (2), 7 (3), 8 sd (2), 9 (5),
        30, 1 (4), 2 (4), 3 (2), 4, 5 (2), 6 (2), 7 (2), 8 (4), 9, 2, var., 40
        (3), 1 (2), 2, 3 var., (5), 4 (3), 5 (3), 6 (9), 7 (2), 8 (5), 9 (3), 50
        (4), 1 (9), 2 (7), 3 (3), 4 (3), 5 (6), 6 (5), 7. Up to 1820 poor,
        others mostly good to v. g. Many varieties.   160 pcs.

HALF CENTS.

743   1793 Fine. Light olive. Rare.
744   1794 Very good. Small head.
745   1795 Thin planchet. Good. Scarce.
746   1797 *Lettered edge.* Fair. Extremely rare.
747   1797 Plain edge. Fair.
748   1800 Very good. Scarce.

749 1802 Very fair. Rare.
750 1803, 4 (2 var.), 5, 6 no stems, 8. Very good.   6 pcs.
751 1804 Crossed 4. Uncirculated. Traces of red.
752 1805 Fine. Light olive. Scarce.
753 1806 Large date, stems to wreath. Extremely fine.
754 1807 Fine. Scarce thus.
755 1809 Uncirculated. Steel color.
756 1810 Good. Scarce.
757 1811 Very good. Rare.
758 1825 Very fine. Light olive.
759 1828 12 stars. Very good.
760 1828 13 stars. Extremely fine. Light olive.
761 1829 Very fine.
762 1831 Altered. Well executed.
763 1832, 3, 4, 5. Very fine.   4 pcs.
764 1849, 50, 1, 3, 4, 5, 6, 7. Very fine.   8 pcs.
765 1793, 4, 5, 7, 1800, 3, 4, 5, 6, 7, 9, 10. 11, 25, 6, 8 (12, 13 stars)
       9, 32, 3, 4, 5, 49, 50, 1, 3, 4, 5, 6, 7. Poor to fine.   32 pcs.
766 1795 2 very poor, 1800, 3, 4 (4), 5, 6 (2), 7 (4), 9 (5), 25, 6 (2),
       8 (5), 9 (2), 32 (3), 3 (5), 4 (2), 5 (6), 49, 50, 1 (3), 3 (2), 4 (2),
       5 (3). Poor to very good.   58 pcs.

PATTERN PIECES OF THE U. S. MINT.

767 1836 FIRST STEAM COINAGE MAR. 23. Bronze. Perfect.
768 1838 Half Doll. Bust of Liberty. R. Flying eagle. Fine.
769 1851 Cent. Liberty seated. Copper. Very fine.
770 1852 Ring dollar. Nickel. Proof.
771 1852 Ring dollar. Copper. Proof.
772 1856 Cent. Flying eagle. Nickel. Very fine. Rare.
773 1858 Cent. Large flying eagle. R. Oak wreath, broad shield.
       Nickel. Proof.
774 1858 Cent. Small flying eagle. R. Same as last. Nickel.
       Proof.
775 1858 Cent. Indian head. R. Same as last. Nickel. Proof.
776 1858 Cent. Indian head. R. Laurel wreath. Nickel. Proof.
777 1866 5 Cents. Bust of Washington, UNITED STATES OF AMERICA.
       R. Wreath enclosing 5 CENTS. Nickel. Proof.
778 1866 5 Cents. Same as last. Copper. Proof.
779 1866 5 Cents. Bust of Washington, IN GOD WE TRUST. R.
       Wreath enclosing 5. Nickel. Proof.
780 1866 5 Cents. Same obv. R. 5 in rays and stars. Nickel.
       Proof. Very rare.

781 1866 5 Cents. Same obv. R. Olive wreath enclosing a large
     5. Copper. Proof.
782 1866 5 Cents. Shield. R. As last. Copper. Proof.
783 1867 5 Cents. Indian head. R. V on shield. Aluminium. Proof.
784 1867 5 Cents. Indian head. R. 5 cents in wreath. Nickel.
     Proof.
785 1869 5 Cents. Obv. as last. R. V in wreath. Nickel. Proof.
786 1869 1 Cent. Same as last. R. I in wreath. Nickel. Proof.
787 1837 Feuchtwanger's composition. Cents. Fine.   6 pcs.

UNITED STATES MINOR COINAGE.

788 1870 Small proof set. 1, 2, 3, 5 cents. Scarce.   4 pcs.
789 1871 Small proof set. 1, 2, 3, 5 cents. Scarce.   4 pcs.
790 1872 Small proof set. 1, 2, 3, 5 cents. Scarce.   4 pcs.
791 1873 Small proof set. 1, 2, 3, 5 cents. Rare.   4 pcs.
792 1874 Small proof set. 1, 3, 5 cents.   3 pcs.
793 1876 Small proof set. 1. 3. 5 cents. Scarce.   3 pcs.
794 1877 Small proof set. 1, 3, 5 cents. Rare.   3 pcs.
795 1878 Small proof set. 1, 3, 5 cents. Rare.   3 pcs.
796 1879 Small proof set. 1, 3, 5 cents.   3 pcs.
797 1880 Small proof set. 1, 3, 5 cents.   3 pcs.
798 1881 Small proof set. 1, 3, 5 cents. Scarce.   3 pcs.
799 1882 Small proof set. 1, 3, 5 cents.   3 pcs.
800 1883 Small proof set. 1, 3, 5 (first two) cents.   4 pcs.
801 1883 Small proof set. Duplicate.   4 pcs.
802 1884 Small proof set. 1, 3, 5 cents.   3 pcs.
803 1885 Small proof set. 1, 3, 5 cents.   3 pcs.
804 1886 Small proof set. 1, 3, 5 cents.   3 pcs.
805 5 cents. 1866–1883 inclusive. 67 rays, fine. 70, 76 Uncir.
     Balance proofs. Desirable and scarce set.   20 pcs.
806 5 cents. 1883 (first two issued). 3 c. 1883. Proofs. 3 pcs.
807 3 cents. 1865–1881 inclusive, 1883, 1876 uncir. Proofs.
     Scarce set.   18 pcs.
808 2 cents. 1864–1873 inclusive. 64, 5, 8, 71 uncirculated. Bal.
     proof. Bright red set.   10 pcs.
809 Cent. 1856 flying eagle. Nickel. Very good. Rare.   .
810 Cent. 1858 Indian head. R. Laurel wreath. Proof.
811 Cent. 1859 Oak wreath and shield on rev. Uncirculated.
812 Cent 1877. Bright red proof. Rare.
813 Cents 1878, 79, 80, 1, 3. Proof.   5 pcs.
814 Cents 1857–1885 (1877 fine). 2 types of 1859. Uncir. 31 pcs.
815 Cents 1877. Very good. Scarce.   13 pcs.

UNITED STATES MEDALS.

BRONZE. VERY FINE. CLOSING NUMBER REFERS TO SIZE.

816 Madison, Jas. Pres. Bust. R. Clasped hands. 40.
817 Johnson, A. Pres. Bust. R. Indian & Columbia, etc. 40.
818 Lincoln, A. Pres. Bust. R. Civilized and uncivilized Indians. 48.
819 Grant, U. S. Pres. Bust. R. I INTEND TO FIGHT, ETC. The splendid Swiss Medal. 38.

MEDALS AWARDED BY CONGRESS TO NAVAL OFFICERS.

820 Jones, J. P., for capture of Serapis, 1779. Bust. R. Engagement. Restrike. 35.
821 Jones, Jacob, for capture of Frolic, 1812. Bust. R. Engagement. 40.
822 Burrows, W., for capture of Boxer, 1813. Tomb. R. Engagement. 40.
823 Perry, O. H., for action on Lake Erie, 1813. Bust. R. Wreath. 38.
824 Macdonough, T., for victory over British fleet, 1814. Bust. R. Engagement. 40.
825 Henley, R., for victory on L. Champlain, 1814. Bust. R. Engagement. 40.
826 Biddle, J., for capture of Penguin, 1815. Bust. R. Engagement. 40.
827 Stewart, C., for capture of Cyane and Levant, 1815. Bust. R. Engagement. 40.
828 For Saving Life. Arms of U. S. R. Sailor rescuing a man from the sea. 40.
829 Wreck of S. S. San Francisco, 1854. Pres. by Phil'a. to Capt's., Crighton, Low and Stouffer. City Arms. 48.

MEDALS AWARDED BY CONGRESS TO ARMY OFFICERS.

830 Washington, Geo., for siege of Boston, 1776. Bust. R. The General and staff watching the British depart. 44.
831 Gates, H., for battle of Saratoga, 1777. Bust. R. Burgoyne surrendering his sword to Gates. 36.
832 Scott, W., for battle of Chippewa and Niagara, 1814. Bust. 40.
833 Jackson, A., for battle of N. O., 1815. Bust. R. Victory, etc. 40.
834 Taylor, Z., for Palo Alto, 1846. Bust. 40.

835 Taylor, Z., for battles in Mexico. Pelican feeding her young.
R. View of battle. Extremely fine specimen of the very
rare medal known as the *Pelican Medal*, given by State of
La. 48.
836 Grant, U. S., for Vicksburg and Chattanooga. Bust. R.
View of Vicksburg and Chattanooga, enclosed by Miss.
River, on which are gunboats. One of the largest medals
ever struck. Rare. 64. Mint price was $8.
837 Grant, U. S. Bust r, by *Morgan*. IN MEMORIAM U. S.
GRANT 1822–1885, THOUGH TO EARTH NO MORE, IN OUR
HEARTS FOREVER. R. The general on a battle-field. Wm.
P. 40.
838 New York. Medal presented by the Governor to Volunteers
in war of the rebellion in pursuance of resolutions of the
Senate and Assembly of the State. Arms. R. Ins. and
blank for recipient's name. Shield shape. Massive, being
50 x 70. Extremely rare and seldom seen.
839 N. Y. For same purpose and presented in like manner as
last, which this probably replaced on account of the unwieldy
size and shape. 24.
840 Washington. Head. R. Head-quarters at Tappan. Brilliant. 22.
841 Washington. Bust. R. Independence Hall. Br. 22.
842 Centnl. of the Battle of Groton Heights. Minute-men inside
a fort. Br. 25.
843 Washington, Scott (Lundy's Lane), etc. Different. Bronze.
Very fine. 12–20.   9 pcs.
844 Jackson, Stonewall. Head. R. List of battles. Wm. 32.
845 Lincoln. Head. R. SHALL BE THEN THENCE FORWARD AND
FOREVER FREE. Silver. Proof. 16.
846 Boston Numismatic So. 1873. Members' medal. Cop. 20.
847 Store cards. Uncirculated. Different.   14 pcs.
848 Massachusetts Charitable Mechanic Association. Award
medals. Different. Very fine. 32.   2 pcs.
849 Masonic. Quarter Century of Liberty Lodge, Cohocton, N.
Y., June 15, 5886. Medal designed by Thos. Warner,
Esq. 100 were struck in bronze and only 1 in the other
metals, none to be sold except to members, dies destroyed.
Bronze proof. 22.
850 Sage's Historical tokens. Complete set. Silvered. 15 pcs.

FOREIGN MEDALS.

Bronze proofs unless otherwise described. Closing figures refer to size.

851   Louis XV. Head r. R. Victory on globe, Fœderum Vindex (The Avenger of Treaties.) Exg., trs. (Fort Mahon captured 1756). Rare medal on the loss of Minorca. 26.

852   Loss of Minorca. ½ length figure of Gen. Blakeney, etc. R. ½ length figure of Adm. Byng; WAS MINORCA SOLD TO B FOR FRENCH GOLD. Brass. Good. Rare. 22.

853   Louis XVI and Marie Antoinette Beautiful busts jugata l. R. Queen with infant on her lap, 19 Dec. 1778. 26.

854   Louis XVI and Marie Antoinette. Beautiful busts vis-a-vis. R. Dolphin with rudder, fleet of ships in background. 4 Nov. 1781. A splendid medal. 39.

855   Louis XVI and Marie Antoinette. Very beautiful busts on either side, by Du Vivier, 1781. A superb medallion. 46.

856   Louis XVI. Head r, crowned with cypress. R. France weeping over an urn, leg. trs. (Weep and avenge him). 21 Jan. 1793. Silver. Rare medal on his execution. 19.

857   Louis XVI, Marie Antoinette and his sister Elizabeth. Exquisite busts jugata r. R. Dates of their execution. See Warner cat., plate VII; Rare. 26.

858   Henry IV, Louis XVI, XVII, Marie Antoinette, Elizabeth, Duke de Berry, Duke Conde. Beautiful medallion busts. R. France pouring incense on a burning altar. Splendid medal in their honor. 36.

859   Napoleon I. Bust full face crowned with lotus flowers. R. Emp. in triumphal car drawn by camels gorgeously caparisoned, passing between Pompey's Pillar and Cleopatra's Needle. Beautiful and remarkable medal on the conquest of Egypt, 1798. 26.

860   Napoleon I. Fine head r, by Jeuffroy. R. The beautiful statue of the Venus de Medici. 26.

861   Napoleon I. Bust l. R. Napoleon I in magnificent imperial robes holding up his son; baptismal font and throne in background. A superb and considered the finest medallion of Napoleon. On the baptism of Nap. II. Slight dent on edge. 43.

862   Napoleon I. Head r. by Droz. R. Napoleon giving his son to France. 26.

863   Napoleon I. Fine head l. R. View of his grave at St. Helena. Very fine. Rare. 26.

864 Hortense, Queen of Holland. 1813. Beautiful head. Inscription in Greek. R. Easel, etc. Gilt. 14.
865 Hortense. Same obv. R. Inscription. 14.
866 Eliza, sister of Napoleon. Very fine head r. R. Monument. "To Eliza by the inhabitants of Montone, on the opening of the new route, 1812." Beautiful. 23.
867 Richard III. Fine bust by *Dassier*. R. Tomb. 26.
868 Charles II. Exquisite bust with long hair, crowned, by *Thos. Simon*. R. Coronation, 1661. Silver. Ex. fine. 19.
869 Geo. II. Bust l. R. Arms and names of battles, QUEBEC at top. Silver. Pierced. Very good. Rare. McLachlan Canadian medals, No. 129. 28.
870 Victoria and royal family. Minute medalets in box. 9 pcs.
871 Eliott, G. A., governor of Gibraltar. Bust. R. Naval battle. Fine. 26.
872 Rubens, P. P. Bust in loose cloak and large hat, by *Hart*. R. His monument at Antwerp, 1840. A grand medal. 45.
873 Calvin, John. Bust in furred gown and scull cap. R. His pulpit at Geneva. Splendid medal of the great divine. 38.
874 Newton, Isaac. Bust r. R. Urania. Very fine. 34.
875 Maria Theresa. Bust. R. Minerva. Fine. 34.
876 Charlotte, Augusta, princess and daughter of George III. Beautiful bust. R. Britannia weeping. Exquisite medal on her death, 1817. 31.
877 Vernon, Admiral. Diff. Ex. lot. 3 small size. 1 pierced. 14 pcs.
878 Dampville, Duke de. Viceroy of France in America, 1644. Bust. R. Arms. Restrike. Very fine. Rare. McLachlan Canadian medals, No. 15. 32.
879 Abd-el-Kader. Fine bust in Arab costume. R. Inscription. 36.
880 Mehemet Ali. Fine bust in Turkish costume. R. Sword. 32.
881 Mehemet Ali. Bust ? face. R. Inscription. Rare. 36.
882 Cathedral of Ypres. Exterior. R. Interior. Beautiful. 31½.
883 Cathedral of Malines. Exterior. R. Interior. Beautiful. 32.
884 Shakespeare. Bust, full face, by *Westwood*. R. Stag drinking from a brook; TO WHICH PLACE A POOR SEQUESTRED STAG, etc. Very fine. Rare. 29.
885 Maria Theresa. Odd medal on the violation of the Pragmatic Sanction, 1742. Brass. Very fine. 27.
886 Gregory XIII. Bust. R. Murder of the Huguenots. Modern copy. 20.
887 Peru. Congress at Lima October 1864. Edge battered. Copper. F 9138. 22.

888 Peter the Great. Fine bust r. R. Views of battles, etc. Different. Splendid set. 30. 19 pcs.

889 Catherine II. Beautiful bust with low cut dress. R. Inscription. 28.

890 Elizabeth. Bust r. R. Battlefield of Kunersdorf. 27.

891 Galerie Metallique. Being a splendid series of the great men of France, each medal having a bust on obv., and date of birth and death on rev. Diff. Extra fine. 26. 38 pcs.

BRITISH WAR MEDALS.

The property of an English gentlemen. All of uniform size of $\frac{22}{16}$ths.

892 Waterloo. Head l., of GEORGE P. REGENT. R. Victory, pedestal inscribed WATERLOO, beneath June 18, 1815, above WELLINGTON. Edge, RALPH BROWNE 71ST REGT. Clasp and silver bar, ribbon. Fine. Rare. Cost £1.5.

893 Waterloo. Miniature of last. Very fine. Rare. 12.

894 First Sikh War, 1845, 6. Head l., of Victoria. R. Victory standing, pile of arms at her feet, ARMY OF THE SUTLEJ; in exg., SOBRAON 1846. Edge, SERGT. MICHL. O'LONERGAN 10TH REGT. Private bars to hold the ribbon. Fine, though nicked. Rare.

895 Second Sikh War, 1848, 9. Punjab Medal. Same obv. as last. R. Surrender of the Sikh Army to Lord Gough, TO THE ARMY OF THE PUNJAB, exg., MDCCCXLIX. Edge, same as last. Fine, small nicks. Private bars to hold ribbon. Rare.

896 Second Burmese War, 1852. Same obv. R. Victory crowning a warrior, clasp PEGU (only clasp issued). Edge, GUNNER JOHN SULLIVAN. HORSE ARTY. Very fine.

897 Same, in every respect except edge, GEO. WARNOCK, GUNNER. "SPHINX."

898 Same design. Clasp NORTHWEST FRONTIER. Edge 3209 PTE. THOMAS BURKE, 32D FOOT. Ribbon. Extremely fine.

899 Same design. Clasp BHOOTAN. Edge, 1028 T. TOBIN. H. MS 55TH. REG. Very fine. Rare.

900 Same design. Clasp JOWAKI 1877–8. Edge. 2742 PTE. THOS. MURTON 51st. FOOT. Very fine. Rare.

901 Service in the Baltic, 1854–5. Head of Victoria. R. Britannia seated, in background forts Sveaborg and Bomarsund. No bar issued. Edge, THOMAS JEFFERIES. Fine. Light nicks. Rare.

902 Crimea, 1855. Arms. Edge, 2961. R. CLAYTON 1ST BN 9TH REGT. Fine. Ribbon.

903 India Mutiny, 1857-8. Head of Victoria. R. Britannia and lion, INDIA, 1857-58. Clasp, CENTRAL INDIA. Edge, MAURICE MULCAHY, 1ST EURN BENGAL FUSRS. Ribbon. F. Nicks.

904 Wars in New Zealand, 1864-6. Bust of Victoria in widow's veil. R. Wreath enclosing 1864-1866, around NEW-ZEALAND, VIRTUTUS HONOR. Edge, 721 BERND WRIGHT, 43D LT. INFTRY. Ribbon and private bar. Very fine. Scarce.

905 New Zealand. Same obv. R. Same but no dates in wreath. Edge, 3186 WM. HANAGAN 59TH FOOT. Very fine. Scarce.

906 Abyssinian War, 1867-8. Bust of Victoria with veil, in a 9 pointed star, in angles a letter of ABYSSINIA. R. Wreath enclosing 712 GUNR. T. BRENNAN 5: BY 25TH BGDE R. A. Crown and swivel with ribbon. Extremely fine. Rare.

907 Ashantee War, 1873-4. Head of Victoria with veil. R. British fighting negroes in a jungle or bush. Clasp, COOMASSIE. Edge, 2152 PTE. R. MORTON, 42D HIGHDS, 1873-74. The 42d Highlanders are the celebrated "Black Watch." Very fine. Extremely rare.

908 South Africa, 1877-8. Head of Victoria. R. Prowling lion, SOUTH AFRICA. Clasp 1877-8. Edge, 527 PTE. J. HOGAN, 88TH FOOT. Ribbon. Fine.

909 South Africa. Same design. Clasp 1877-8-9. Edge, 701. PTE. MAGEE, 88TH FOOT. Very fine. Ribbon.

910 South Africa. Same design. Clasp, 1879. Edge 2279. PTE. J. CASEY, 91ST FOOT. Very fine.

911 Afghanistan, 1878-80. Bust of Victoria with crown and veil and title of Empress. R. Elephant carrying a cannon surrounded by a guard of native troops. Edge, 457. PTE. P. MURPHY 1/5TH FUSRS. Extremely fine.

912 Afghanistan, 1878-80. Same design. Edge, 10B/119. PTE. T. HARRINGTON 2/14TH REGT. Very fine.

913 Afghanistan, 1878-80. Same design. Edge, 69B/2328. PTE P. TARPE, 1/18TH REGT. Fine.

914 Afghanistan, 1878-80. Same design. Edge, 1744. PTE. J. POWER, 85TH FOOT. Very fine.

915 Egyptian Campaign. Head with veil, etc. R. Sphinx, EGYPT 1882. Clasp, TEL-EL-KEBIR. Edge, 1151 SERGT. J. MC GRATH. 1/R. I. FUS. Ribbon. Extremely fine.

916 Egyptian Campaign. Same in every respect, having clasp. Edge. 2255 PTE E. FALVEY 2/R. IR. R. Very fine.

917 Egyptian Campaign. Same in every respect. Edge, 2420. PTE A. SHEA 2/ YORK & LANC. R. Very good. Nicked.

918 Egyptian Campaign. Same, but without clasp. Edge, PTE. J. BIBBY, 2/ DERBY. R. Fine.

919 Egyptian Campaign. Bronze star and bar. Sphinx and pyramids; EGYPT, 1882. R. Khedive's monogram crowned. Ribbon. Perfect.

920 Egyptian Campaign. Same. Slightly rubbed.

921 Long Service. Arms. R. FOR LONG SERVICE AND GOOD CONDUCT. Edge, 3011. J. CARROLL 87TH FOOT. Ribbon. Very fine. Rare.

922 Long Service. Same design. Edge, 3562. GUNNER P. MCDONALD, 11TH Bde R. A. Very fine. Rare.

922a Ribbons for Ghuznee, 1839. Crimea and China (2). 4 pcs.

923 France. Louis XVIII. Large fleur-de-lis, bearing small medallion of LOUIS XVIII, suspended from crown and ring. Perfect. Rare. 10 x 15.

924 France. Louis XVIII. Fleur-de-lis, suspended from crown and ring. Perfect. 14 x 6.

925 France. "The Medal of July." Gallic cock on tricolor. Leg., trs., "A grateful country to its defenders." R. 3 wreaths, leg. trs., "Our country and liberty." 27-28-29 July, 1830. Edge, trs., "Presented by the King of the French." Crown and ring. Very fine. Rare. 15.

926 Papal States. Pius IX. 1849. Bronze. Ribbon. Perfect. 20.

COLLECTION OF COINS.

THE PROPERTY OF

N. L. McDONALD, Esq.,

NEWARK, N. Y.

AMERICAN COLONIAL AND STATE COINS.

927 1652 Mass. Pine-tree three pence. Pierced. Fair.
928 (1681) N. J. Mark Newby farthing. Fair.
929 1722 Rosa Americana. Uncrowned rose. Penny. Fair.
930 1773 Virginia. Geo. III. Bust. ½ penny. Fine.
931 1781 North American token. Very good.
932 1787 New York. Bust r. NOVA EBORAC. R. Liberty r. V. g.
933 1787 U. S. Cent. Sun dial. FUGIO. R. 13 links, etc. Good.
934 1794 N. Y. Talbot, Allum & Lee Cent. Very fine.
935 1794 N. Y. Same obv. R. Bust of John Howard. Good.
936 1721 La., Mass., N. J., Conn., Vt., etc. Poor. 10 pieces.
937 1783 Washington Cent. Bust l. UNITY STATES. Fine.
938 1783 Washington Cent. Bust l. R. Liberty seated. V. g.
939 (1783) Washington Cent. Head on either side. V. g.

UNITED STATES CENTS.

940 1795 Thin planchet. ONE CENT high in wreath. Good.
941 1800 Erroneous die. 79 under 80. Very good.
942 1805 Fair.
943 1812 Good.
944 1814 Plain 4. Very good.
945 1821 Very good. Surface slightly corroded.
946 1823 over 1822. Good. Scarce.
947 1826 With inner line. Fine. Dark color.
948 1827 Fine. Surface oxidized. Dark color.
949 1833 Very fine. Light brown color.
950 1847 Extremely fine. Light olive.
951 1856 Slanting 5. Uncirculated. Light olive.
952 Set 1793–1857. 1793 chain, v. poor. 1793 wreath, etc., 1793
      Liberty cap, poor, shows date. 1804 restrike, 1809, 1811
      poor. No. 1799. Varieties and a few duplicates. Poor to
      good.   100 pcs.
953 Set 1857 to 1885. Very good to uncirculated.   30 pcs.

954 Half cents. 1795 v. poor, 1803, 5, 7, 9, 25, 8, 9, 32, 5, 55. Poor
     to good.   11 pcs.
955 1834 Token. Ship to r. FELLOW CITIZENS SAVE YOUR CON-
     STITUTION. R. Liberty cap, radiated ; THE GLORIOUS WHIG
     VICTORY OF 1834. Copper. Extremely fine. Rare.
956 1837 Tokens. Different. Very good.   21 pcs.
957 1838 Slave kneeling. AM I NOT A WOMAN. Very fine.
958 Rebellion tokens. V. g. Includes the scarce "spoot." 38 pcs.

FOREIGN COPPER COINS.

959 Africa, Portugese. Peter V. ½ Macuta, 1858. Very fine.
960 Africa. Liberia. Cent, 1833. 2 cents and cent 1847–62.
     Very good.   3 pcs.
961 Africa. Sierra Leone Co. Prowling lion. Penny 1791. V. f.
962 Africa. Same device. Cent, 1791. Beautiful bronze proof.
963 Argentine Republic. Liberty head. 2 centavos, 1883. V. f.
964 Barbadoes. Negro head. R. Neptune. Penny, 1792. Fine.
965 Brunswick. Wild man and tree. Pfennig, 1776. Very good.
966 Burmah. Thebau. Peacock. Very good and scarce.
967 Cambodia. Norodom I. Palace tokens for 10, 15, 20, 25
     centimes. Brass proofs.   4 pcs.
968 Canada. Includes Magdalen Is. token. Av. good. 64 pcs.
969 Ceylon. Geo. III. Bust. R. Elephant. ½ 1, 2 stivers,
     1815. Fine.   3 pcs.
970 Ceylon. Elephant. 192, 96, 48 to one rupee, 1802. Very
     good, one a proof.   3 pcs.
971 Cochin China. Fig. of France seated. 1 cent and Cash 1879.
     Brilliant red. Rare.   2 pcs.
972 Dominica. Centavo, 1877. Brass. Uncirculated.
973 Egypt. Glass money. Fine specimen.
974 England. Geo. III. Bust. 2 pence. Large. Very good.
975 England. ¼, ¼, ¼, ¼ farthing, penny. Very g., to unc. 7 pcs.
976 England. ½ penny tokens. Poor to very fine.   23 pcs.
977 England. Revolutionary ½ penny token 1790. Man standing.
     J. SPENCE SLOP SELLER NEW CASTLE. R. Shepherd under a
     tree. Proof.
978 England. Lady Godiva. ½ penny 1792. Very good.
979 England. Norwich. View of Castle. ½ penny 1794. Red.
980 England. Farthing tokens. Uncir. Diff. Splendid lot. 25 pcs.
981 France. Nap. III, seated on cannon and skulls. Satirical
     token, 1868. Proof.
982 Guernesey. Arms. 8 doubles, 1858. Uncirculated.

983 Honduras. View of Island. ⅛, ¼ real, 1869. Nickel. Uncirculated. 2 pcs.
984 Hungary. Republic under Rakoczy. 5, 10 Kr. 1706. Very good. 2 pcs.
985 Ionian Is. Winged lion. ¼, ½, 1 obolo. Very good. 3 pcs.
986 Isle of Man. 1733, 1758. Poor and good. 3 pcs.
987 Italy. Napoleon I. Head. Centesimo. Uncirculated.
988 Jamaica. Victoria. ¼, ½, 1 penny, 1869, 80. Nickel. V g. 3 pcs.
989 Morocco. Sidi Mohammed. Dated, 1286-1869. 3 Falus. Fine.
990 Mysore. Elephant l. Fair.
991 New Foundland. Victoria. Bust. Cent, 1880. Semi-proof. Red.
992 Russia. Nicholas I. 5, 10 Kopecks, 1831-7. Uncirculated. Red. 2 pcs.
993 Russia, Portugal, Papal States, Sicily, etc. All large. Very good. 25 pcs.
994 Sandwich Is. Kamehameha III. Bust. Cent, 1847. V. g.
995 Sarawak. J. and C. Brooke. ½, 1 cent. Fine. 3 pcs.
996 Scotland. Chas. II. Also Elizabeth for Ireland. Poor. 3 pcs.
997 Servia. Milan IV. 10 para. 1879. Uncirculated.
998 Siam. Fuang. 1874. Fine. Light scratches.
999 Siberia. Catherine II. Sables and shield. *Edge lettered.* 10 Kopecks, 1766. Fine. Very rare.
1000 Siberia. Same device. Edge not lettered. 1, 2 Kop., 1771-9. Very good. 2 pcs.
1001 Spain. Philip IV. Head. 8, 16 maravedi, 1663. Gd. 2 pcs.
1002 Straits Settlements. Victoria. ¼, ½, 1 cent. 1872. V. g. 3 pcs.
1003 Sumatra. Sultana. Kepengs. 1804. Very fine. 2 pcs.
1004 Surinam. Parrot. 4 Duit, 1679. R. Blank. Very good.
1005 Sweden. Adolphus Frederick. ½ daler, 1758. Square plate with 5 counterstamps. Fine specimen of this strange coinage. Rare. 56 x 54.
1006 Tunis. Abd-el-Aziz. 1, 2, 4, 8 Kharubs. Very gd. 4 pcs.
1007 Tuscany. Prov. Gov. 1, 2, 5 Centesimi, 1859. V. g. 3 pcs.
1007a Placque. Bust l. CYRUS REX PERSARUM. Bronze. 62.
1008 Balance of the collection. Good and very good. Great variety. 310 pcs.
1009 Another lot. Poor. Some fair. 378 pcs.
1010 Pierced, damaged and very poor coins of the coll. 62 pcs.
1011 Base silver. Poor to very good. 50 pcs.
1012 Africa. Sierra Leone Co. Silver, 10 cents, 1805. V. good.
1013 England. Edward I. Silver penny. Good.
1014 Japan. Silver, ¼ itzbue. Oblong. Uncirculated.
1015 Mexico. Maximilian. Silver 5 cents 1864. Very fine.

1016 Newfoundland, etc. 20-cent size. Good.   6 pcs.
1017 Various. Dime size. Good. 5 pierced.   30 pcs.
1018 Various. ½ dime size. Includes Ionian Is. 6 pierced.
      Good.   32 pcs.
1019 Dye's Coin Encyclopædia. Numerous illustrations. 1152
      pp. 8vo. Cloth. New. Philada., 1883.
1020 Coin Catalogues. Some priced. Coin Journal July 1883 to
      December 1884.   55 pcs.

U. S. FRACTIONAL CURRENCY.

Uncirculated, unless otherwise stated.

1021 First issue. 10 cents. Washington. Perforated edges. R.
      Slightly soiled. Rare.
1022 First issue. Dupl. Same condition. Without AB Co. Rare.
1023 First issue. 5, 10, 25 cents. Unperforated edges. AB Co. 3 pcs.
1024 Second issue. 5, 10 cents. Head of Washington in gilt
      ring.   2 pcs.
1025 Second issue. 50 cent. Obv. has only gilt ring. R. As
      issued. Another with only the gilt work. Soiled. Unique.
      2 oddities.   2 pcs.
1026 Third issue. 10 cents. Washington. Autograph signatures
      of Colby and Spinner. Red back.
1027 Third issue. 10 cents. Same printed signatures. Red back.
      Very fine.
1028 Third issue. 10 cents. Same, but with green back.
1029 Third issue. 25 cent. Fessenden. Red back. Ex. f. Scarce.
1030 Fourth issue. 10 cents. Liberty. Varieties.   4 pcs.
1031 Fifth issue. 10 cents. Meredith. Green seal. Scarce.
1032 Fifth issue. 10, 25, 50 cents.   3 pcs.
1033 Rebellion envelopes. A choice collection, containing 8
      Confederates, 69 in bronze (nearly all views), balance in
      colors. Different. Clean.   346 pcs.
1034 Rebellion envelopes. Duplicates. 25 in bronze.   29 pcs.
1035 Foreign copper coins. Liberia. George III. 2 p. (pierced).
      Mexico, Peru, etc. Some base silver. Good.   190 pcs.
1036 American Journal of Numismatics, Vol. I (1866) to Vol.
      XVI (1882), inclusive. In parts. Clean. Very rare and
      valuable. Seldom offered. 16 Vols.
1037 Batty's English Copper Tokens. A most exhaustive treatise
      of the subject. In parts from Nos. 1 to 29, 1868–1884, in-
      clusive. New. Rare. Seldom offered. Right to subscribe
      to succeeding numbers sold with it. 29 parts.

www.ingramcontent.com/pod-product-compliance
Lightning Source LLC
Chambersburg PA
CBHW020817030726
47496CB00009B/2925